a **Poppy** and **Max** book

ORCHARD BOOKS

Here Come Poppy and Max

Lindsey Gardiner

For my Mum and Dad –
you're simply the best

 ORCHARD BOOKS

ORCHARD BOOKS
96 Leonard Street, London EC2A 4XD
Orchard Books Australia
Unit 31/56 O'Riordan Street, Alexandria, NSW 2015
ISBN 1 84121 357 8 (Hardback)
ISBN 1 84121 600 3 (Paperback)
First published in Great Britain in 2000
First paperback publication in 2001
Text and illustrations © Lindsey Gardiner 2000
The right of Lindsey Gardiner to be identified as the author
and illustrator of this work has been asserted by her in accordance
with the Copyright, Designs and Patents Act, 1988.
A CIP catalogue for this book is available from the British Library.
(Hardback) 10 9 8 7 6 5 4 3 2 1
(Paperback) 10 9 8 7 6 5 4 3 2
Printed in Singapore

This is
Poppy.

This is
Max.

Poppy wants to be like
all her favourite animals.   She. . .

walks tall

like a giraffe,

splashes

like a duck,

waddles

like a penguin,

roars

like a tiger,

leaps

like a leopard,

stands on
one leg

like a flamingo,

bounces

like a kangaroo, but. . .

. . .her favourite animal of all
is Max, her dog.

And he loves Poppy
just the way she is.

Bye
bye

See you again soon. . .